Thomas' Trusty Wheels

Based on
The Railway Series
by the
Rev. W. Awdry

Illustrations by
Robin Davies

EGMONT

Spencer was puffing proudly down the Main Line, when suddenly there was a **HISS**! Spencer had to stop – he had burst a safety valve!

The Duke was worried. "How are we going to get to Callan Castle on time now?" he sighed.

Thomas soon caught up with Spencer.

"Have your **twenty** wheels stopped working already?" he teased.

Spencer frowned. Now Thomas would have to take the Duke and Duchess to the ball! They climbed on board, and Thomas puffed away.

"**Six** wheels to the rescue!" Thomas smiled.

Thomas hadn't gone far when he had to stop, too. Just around the bend, a tree had fallen across the tracks.

"Cinders and ashes!" Thomas cried, as he screeched to a halt.

"Sorry," Thomas called to the Duke and Duchess. "But we can't carry on."

Before long, Bertie beeped by. **"Toot! Toot!"**
Thomas showed him the tree on the line.

"Four wheels are best," Bertie boasted. "I'll take
the Duke and Duchess by road!"

So the Duke and his wife climbed on board.

Next, it was Bertie's turn to stop, when his front tyres rolled over some pins, **POP! POP!**

The Thin Controller was passing, on his bicycle.

"I'll go and fetch help," he said. "You can trust **two** wheels!"

And off he rode to find a telephone box.

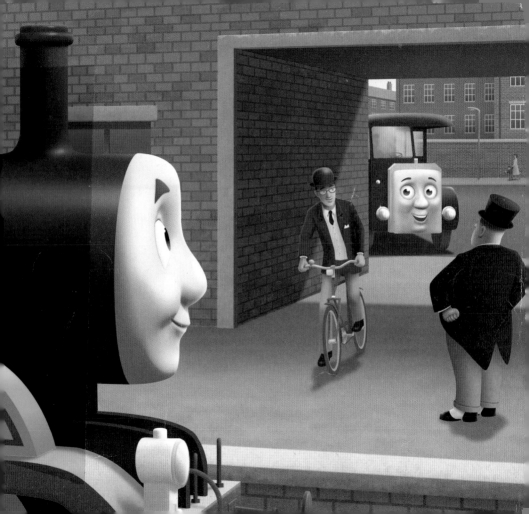

"**Two** wheels?" Bertie beeped. "Everybody knows that **four** wheels are best!"

"How can **four** wheels be better than **six**?" Thomas replied.

Just then, Spencer steamed in. "**Twenty** wheels are the best, by far!" he boomed.

They were still arguing when Spencer remembered he had to hurry to the birthday ball.

Minutes later, Harold came buzzing overhead. He landed safely next to Bertie.

"Hop on board!" Harold called to the Duke and Duchess. "I'll get you to Callan Castle."

Holding onto their hats, they climbed into Harold's cockpit, then Harold **whirred** away.

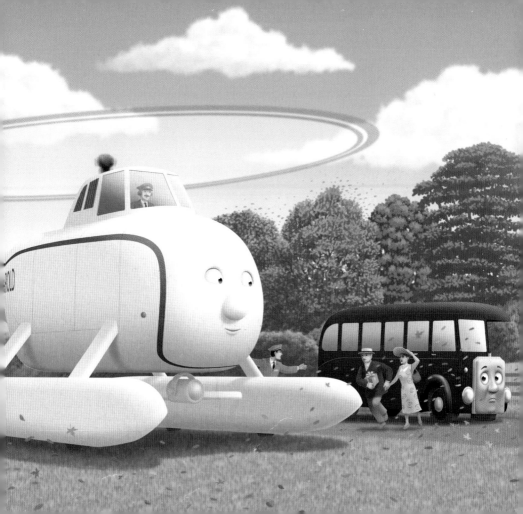

By the evening, Spencer's safety valve had been fixed, Rocky had cleared the tracks for Thomas and Bertie had new tyres.

"What a day!" said Thomas. "And we still don't know how many wheels are best."

Suddenly, there was a **whirring** noise in the sky.

It was Harold, on his patrol.

Thomas smiled. "It was Harold who saved the day," he peeped. "And he didn't use **any** wheels!"

"Hooray for helicopters!" Spencer cheered.

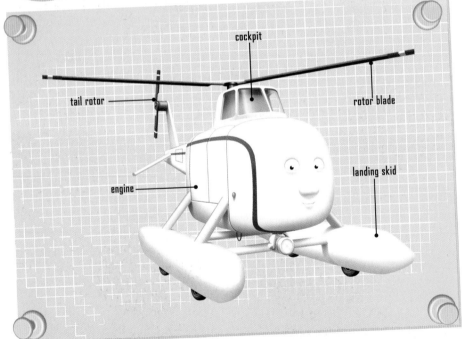

tail rotor

cockpit

rotor blade

engine

landing skid

Harold's challenge to you

Look back through the pages of this book
and see if you can spot:

sign

ducks

weather vane

present

Bus Driver

THE *THOMAS* ENGINE ADVENTURES

 Thomas
 Percy
 Harold
 James
 Cranky
 Spencer

 Gordon
 Flynn
 Toby
 Henry
 Hiro
 Emily

 Thomas and Bertie's Race
 Thomas Goes Crash!
 Kevin
 Diesel
 Troublesome Trucks
 Charlie

 The Thomas Way
 Thomas' New Friend
 Oliver
 Victor
 Thomas' Trusty Wheels
 Thomas Helps Hiro

EGMONT